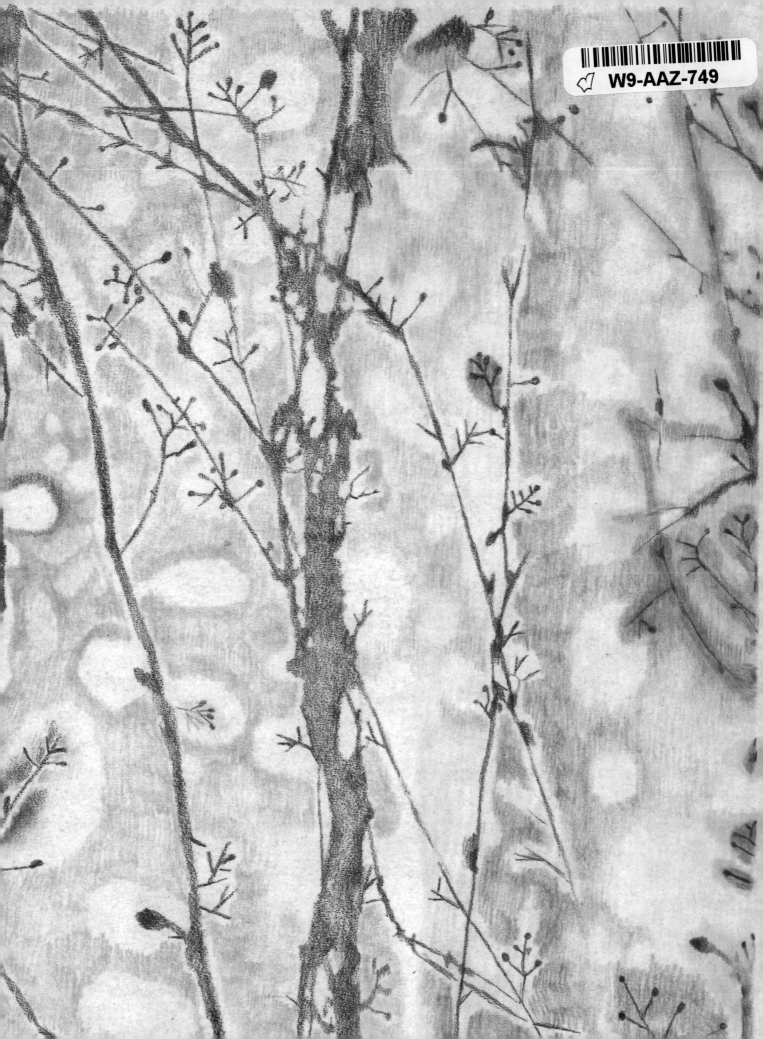

For Nahid, without whom there could have been no departure,
and for Claudia, without whom there would have been no arrival. — J.L.

To all of you who like picture books chock full of details, as I did as a child. — N.K.

www.enchantedlion.com

First published in 2019 by Enchanted Lion Books,
67 West Street, 317A, Brooklyn, NY 11222

Text copyright © 2019 by JonArno Lawson
Illustrations copyright © 2019 by Nahid Kazemi

ISBN 978-1-59270-262-6

Printed in China

First Printing

Over The Rooftops, Under The Moon

JonArno Lawson   Nahid Kazemi

ENCHANTED LION BOOKS
NEW YORK

You can be far away inside,

and far away outside.

With others, but still on your own

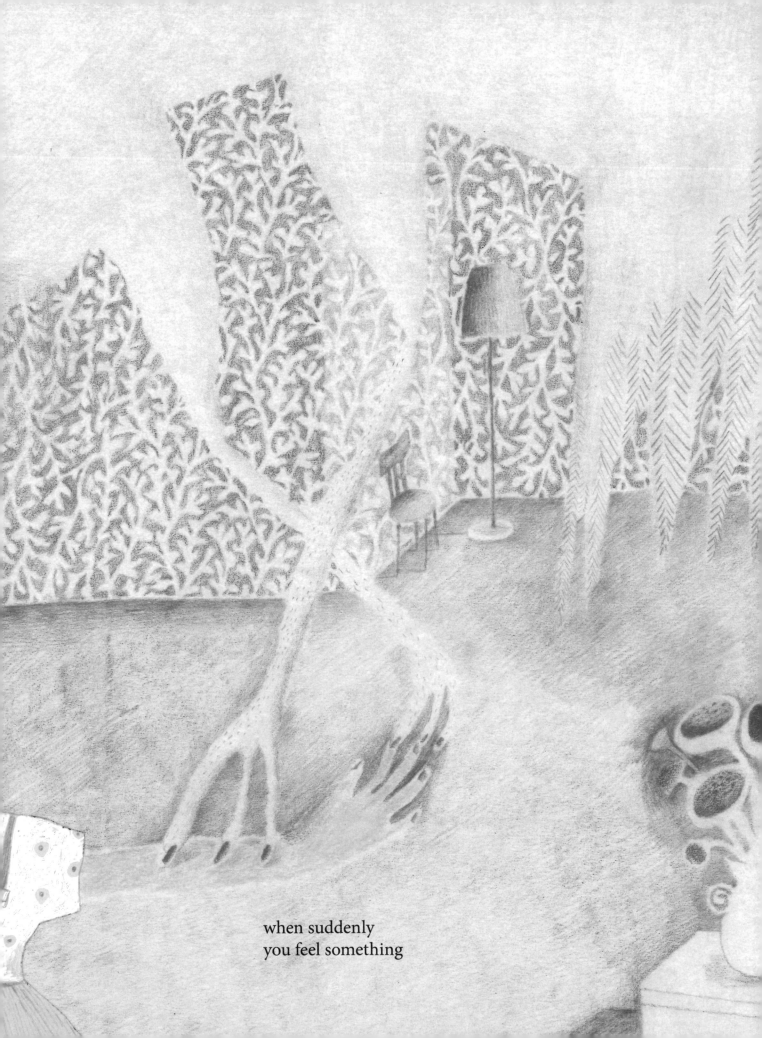

when suddenly
you feel something

that gets you moving

and wondering

about life.

All of it.

Color arrives,
sometimes when
you least expect it.

But then snow falls

and something
changes again.

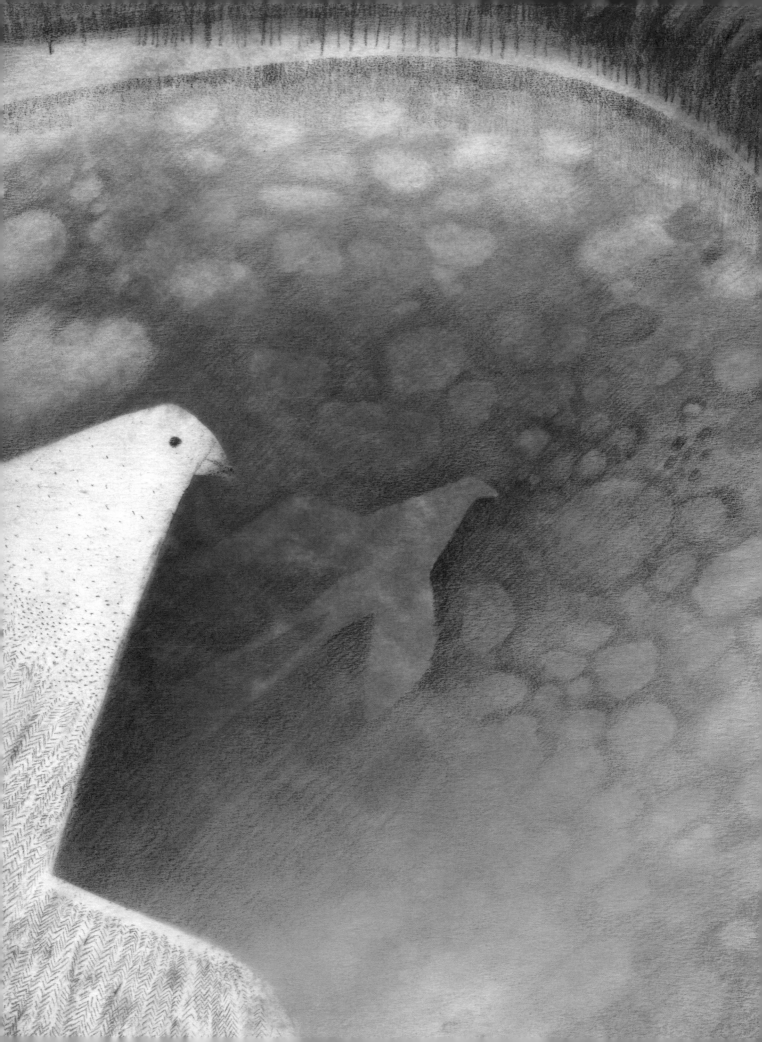

Where are the others now?

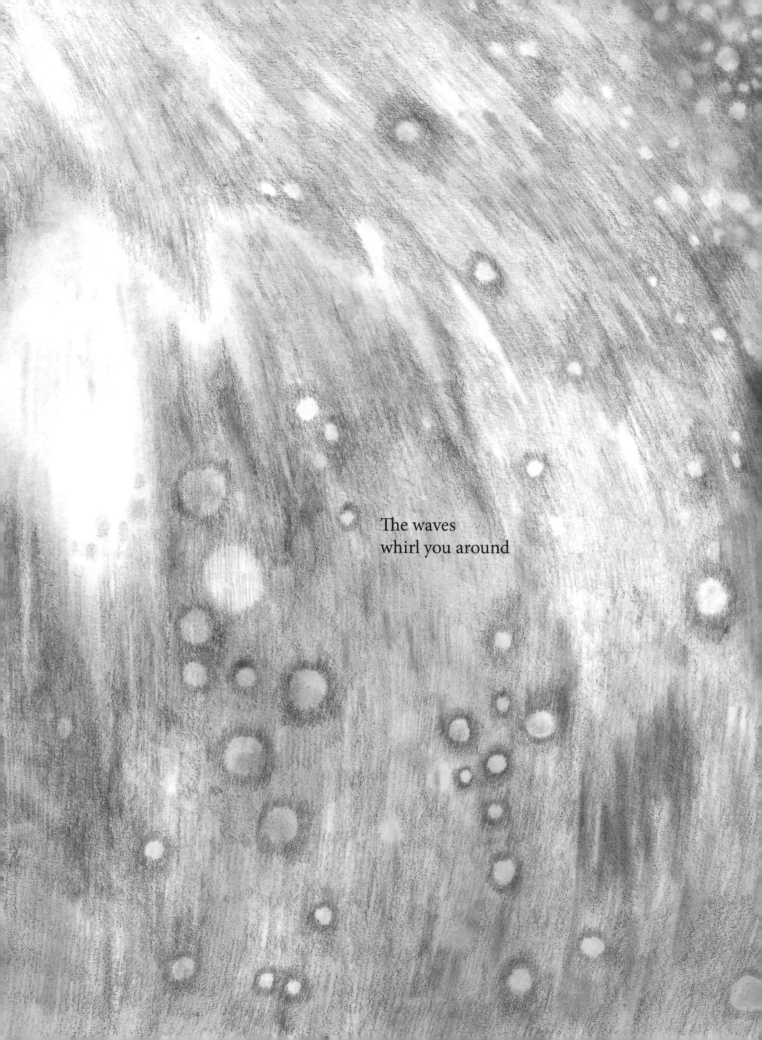

The waves
whirl you around

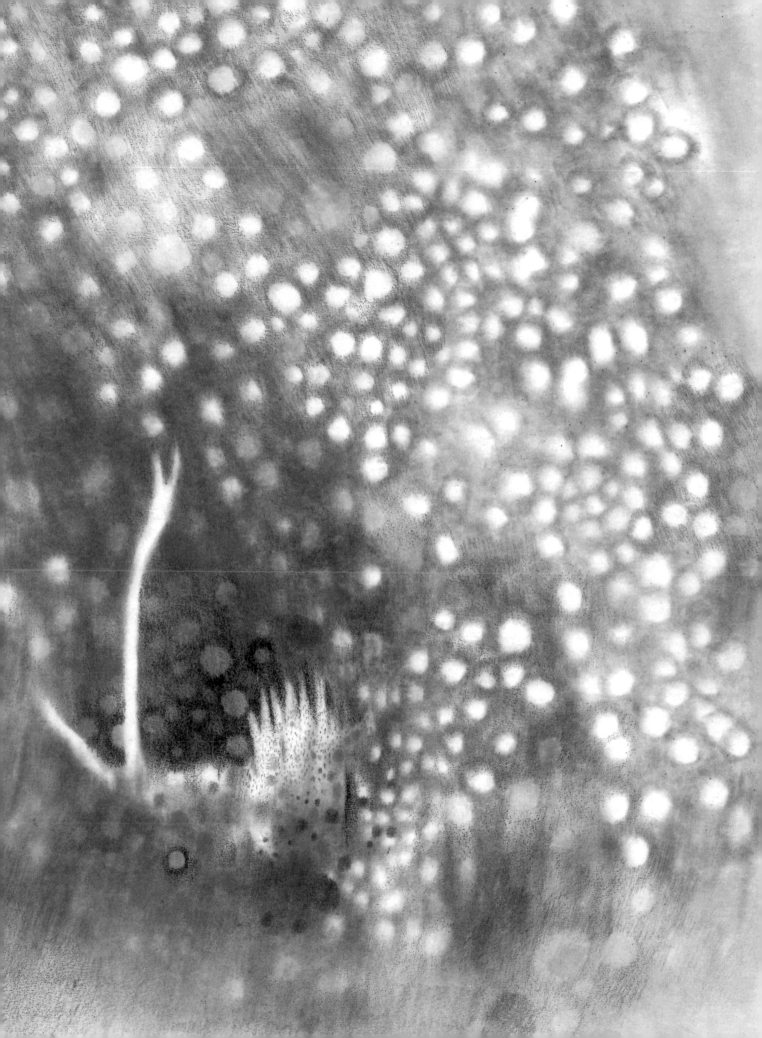

to a leaf
that carries you ashore

to somewhere
very familiar.

Inside and outside

alone and together

over the rooftops

and under the moon.